For Bella and Perrin, our greatest inspirations.
You can be anything that you want to be!

Love, Mom & Dad

IMPRINT
A part of Macmillan Publishing Group, LLC
175 5th Avenue, New York, NY 10010

ABOUT THIS BOOK
The art in this book was created digitally. The text was set in Filson Soft.
This book was edited by Erin Stein and designed by Natalie C. Sousa.
The production was supervised by Raymond Ernesto Colón, and the production editor was Dawn Ryan.

Our books may be purchased in bulk for promotional, educational, or business use. Please contact your local bookseller
or the Macmillan Corporate and Premium Sales Department at (800) 221-7945 ext. 5442
or by e-mail at MacmillanSpecialMarkets@macmillan.com.

Library of Congress Cataloging-in-Publication Data is available.
ISBN 978-1-250-13857-6

Imprint logo designed by Amanda Spielman

First Edition, 2018

1 3 5 7 9 10 8 6 4 2

mackids.com

If thee be a Pirate, this book do not plunder,
or ye shall find yerself six feet under!
If thou be a Princess, be gracious, be fair.
If thou stealest this book, of the dungeons beware!

Eleanor Wyatt
Princess and Pirate

written by **Rachael MacFarlane**   illustrated by **Spencer Laudiero**

{Imprint}
MAKE YOUR MARK

New York

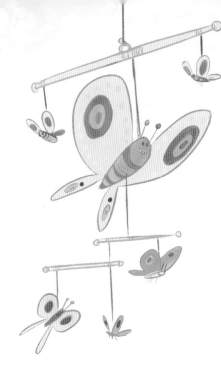

My name is Eleanor—
Eleanor Wyatt.

Some days I'm a princess.
Some days I'm a pirate!

I live in a castle, the best in the land!

It's also a fort for my swashbuckling band.

I have fifteen teapots
for serving my tea,

and I don't spill a drop
when I sail the high seas.

I can sword fight the scariest
bad guys in town,

then I twirl to the ball
in my finest ball gown.

My high heels can sparkle
in the warm summer sun,

but I kick them off
when I'm ready to run.

I must wear my crown when I go to the park,

then I switch to my cape when it starts to get dark.

My mom says I don't have to play just one way.

My dad says there's no right or wrong way to play.

My tutus are fluffy and twirly and pink!

My ninja gi's blacker than the blackest black ink!

I'm awaiting my prince
while trapped in a tower.

Then I'm saving the world
with my superpower.

My friends and I like to play different things.
We're cowboys and monsters and fairies with wings.

Let your inner light shine, and be who you are.
Let your friends do the same, and you'll shine like a star!

My dad tucks my dolls
all cozy in bed.

Mom puts my monster mask
snug on my head.

I can be anything that I want to be!

I'm a princess, a pirate . . .

but I'm also just me.